DEVOTION

DEVOTION

written by

K.J. STEVENS

Published by
CROOKED STEEPLE PRESS

ISBN: 979-8-9986462-0-1

CROOKED STEEPLE PRESS
thecrookedsteeple.com
Alpena, MI 49707

STORIES

lasting

Another day of computer screens and spreadsheets. Emails and conference calls. More of my life sucked away into the gray fabric of cubicle walls. I have grown to hate my job, but doing so has only made me hate myself a little too. There are people working harder in worse places—in ditches and caves, on rooftops, and in graves—so I shouldn't complain. I have company-paid health insurance, accumulate company-matched dollars in a 401k, and make enough money so ends not only meet, but overlap. This allows me the comfort of indulgence, so I can make these trips like this—to the Galilee Lake Grocery Store.

It's Friday, 5:33 pm, and December dark in Thunder Bay, Michigan. Freezing rain has started and is laying a slippery base for the eight inches of heavy, wet snow that's yet to come. I just want to get in. Get out. Get home. Open a fresh bottle, pour a tall glass, and watch a mindbender I've seen before. Maybe *Fight Club, Magnolia,* or *Donnie Darko.* But the place is packed. It's a meat puppet zoo. Shoppers dazed by the drop in

10

barometric pressure and mesmerized by the buzz of flickering fluorescent lights are loading up on shit they don't need, as if it's the end of the world. Two of them, slow and fat, waddle along in front of me. Their black sweatshirts and camouflage pajama pants wrestle with bulges and stretch to the max, testing the tensile strength of Bangladesh-threaded seams. Before I get too far down the dark hole of judgment, I remind myself—we all have issues, challenges, demons inside. And just maybe they're here for a healthy start—leafy greens, cruciferous vegetables, berries, and legumes. Coconut water, herbal tea, kombucha. As I maneuver around them I see that their cart is loaded to the gills. Hot dogs, potato chips, easy cheese. Donuts, ice cream, Oreos, Pop-Tarts, and Mountain Dew. They reek of hard-to-reach dirty places and weed, and as I pass them, they break out into a game of hot potato with a jar of brown gravy. Like idiots, they toss it back and forth until there's a miss and it falls and bursts into a caramel-colored mess of corn syrup solids, modified milk ingredients, and glass shards

11

all over the floor. They laugh like hyenas, do an about-face, and stroll on.

A garbled voice crackles to life on the loudspeaker and summons Matthew. He blasts through the silver swinging doors at the back of the store pushing a squeaky-wheeled mop bucket. He's tall and thin. Has jet black hair, glossy pink fingernails, holes in the knees of his blue jeans, and a purple tiger lily tattoo on the right side of his neck. We cross paths at an endcap of noodles—elbows, penne, and rotini. I give him a nod. He glides past as if I'm invisible, whistling *Somewhere over the Rainbow*. I grab a can of SPAM, a loaf of white bread, a jar of jalapenos, and a package of processed sliced cheese singles then weave my way through the faceless bodies until I reach The Liquor Cubby. As usual, it shines. The vibrant colors and seductive shapes quicken my pulse. Provocative labels tempt me. I bite my lip and gaze over the shelves with awe. Today, however, I'm not here to get carried away, swayed by big budget advertising or slick slogans. This isn't a midweek

12

purchase—a top shelf sipper to take the edge off and nudge me to sleep. This is weekend drinking. Quantity over quality. So, a half-gallon of Burnett's will do.

Light-footed, full of hope, I carry the bottle under my arm like a baby until I reach checkout four. I find myself waiting behind a tiny, wrinkled man. His brown wool coat looks too big for him, the shoulders sagging. The matching hat is pulled down, nearly hiding rhinestone-studded spectacles that ride low on his nose. Grapes and chocolate milk. Cottage cheese, raisins, and toilet paper. A family-size bag of peppermint patties and nine cans of soup. Six chicken, one French onion, and two cream of mushroom. Each beep over the barcode scanner is a metronome, marking time with precision.

And then he plunks one more item onto the counter: a giant bottom-shelf bottle of vodka. Burnett's, of course. He notices me and my bottle, and grins. His teeth are gray, uneven, tired. I try to look away, but there's something in his expression—half amusement, half something I can't name—that holds me. *Paper or plastic*, the cashier asks. He chooses paper. Has coupons for everything. His thin, veiny fingers tremble as he pulls out a checkbook from his coat. His hand shakes. He asks for today's date. Then he writes the total. In cursive. Laboring over every letter and digit, as if stretching the moment will stretch the hours of his day, the years of his life, making all of this last.

His hands, the weight of the coat, the way gravity is slowly, inevitably pulling him into the earth—they feel familiar. The fluorescent lights flicker, bending the edges of reality. The air around us is charged, like the moment before a storm breaks. I glance down at my own hands gripping the bottle and see something different—a slight tension, a tremor never there before. It spreads like static through my chest. Steals my breath, and I gasp. The old man doesn't notice. His fingers continue scratching slowly, deliberately, as if no one is waiting, as if he's alone.

The cashier hands him his receipt. He shuffles forward, the paper bag cradled in his arms, the blue top of the Burnett's peeking out like a flag planted in ruins. He turns his head slightly, just enough to grin once more. His eyes catch the light, sliver-rimmed in weariness, and I see myself. A whisper of a future I don't want to face but can't ignore.

starlite

The sky flashes and thunder grumbles. Reverend Romanowski is sober for now but moves us along with urgency. Not because of the threatening weather, but because thirty yards away, near the grill pits, public showers, and toilets, there's a covered pavilion. Under it, there's enough alcohol for two hundred people. We are expecting seventy-five.

"The challenge of your journey is to remember. Love is not greedy or jealous. Lustful or carnal. It does not require blessings, a contract, or vows. It exists and thrives, grows and lasts, because of faithfulness. Understanding. Grace."

The Reverend pauses. Looks over his shoulder at the wide swath of gray gliding across the bay. Lightning flickers. I count— *one-one-thousand, two-one-thousand, three-one-thou...*

"Love," he says, "is friendship in its purest form—devotion."

I'm marveling at the billowy dark clouds, taken by their fury, when Maggie squeezes my hand. She brings me back to us. Starlite Beach. Barefoot in the sand. The sky breaking, and rain christening our first kiss as husband and wife.

The Reverend covers his bald head with his worn, leather-bound Bible and hightails it toward the party. He is tall. Broad-shouldered. Heavy-set, but moves quickly. His long easy strides remind onlookers he was once the town's most gifted athlete, setting unbreakable high school records in football, basketball, and track. When he reaches the pavilion, he's met with open arms by Elwood, Maggie's Dad. Stout with a bushy snow-white beard and mustache, he's wearing a white suit, big white Stetson, and blue suede cowboy boots. Their embrace is odd. Lasts a little too long. Like long-lost lovers or reunited war brothers. When they finally part, red-faced, wiping their eyes, the Reverend pulls a flask from inside his coat, and they drink.

Maggie holds my hands. Gazes over the lake as rain falls in great, gray slanted sheets. Seagulls dot the beach and bob atop waves. A lone Canadian goose swims slowly in a circle near a crooked willow that reaches out over the water.

"I'm going to miss this place," she says.

"Not me. We need to get out so we can do what we're meant to do."

"And what's that?"

"Write and paint and make babies."

"You're pretty sure of yourself."

"I'm sure of us," I say.

We kiss. My heart pounds. It's like this a lot with her—everything always feeling new.

A gaggle of old ladies huddled under the pavilion near the horseshoe pits, smoking and drinking, watches us. They look familiar, but only in the way people do if you stare too long. They could be great aunts or distant cousins. I don't know and don't care. They pop umbrellas in unison, link arms, then start toward us, waving and smiling.

"Aw, Christ. Not now," I say.

Maggie grabs my newly ringed finger. Tugs.

"Be nice!"

Thankfully, lightning strikes. So close and so violent that it sends them waddling back to shelter.

Maggie stares into the sky.

"I smell ozone," she says.

"I think that's burnt hair and dirty diapers."

"You're awful!"

She shoves me, laughs, and we run. From the beach, through the thick wet grass and puddles, past the swings and teeter-totters, to the reception—an event so overdone I can barely stand it. Silver centerpieces, monogrammed napkins, frilly tablecloths. Gaudy decorations and assigned seating for friends and family attending not out of love and support—we haven't seen these people in years—but for the catered meal. Prime rib and walleye from Thunder Bay's finest restaurant, Jack's Sawmill. And most importantly, an open bar stocked with kegs from Lumber Brothers Brewery, wine from Thunder Bay Winery, and booze from Sunnyside Distillery.

"Quite the show," I say.

"That's Dad," she says. "Elwood, the showman."

Guests gather at tables and cluster in cliques. They're drinking. Catching up. Killing time while they wait for us. We walk around back of the pavilion and sneak in behind the bar to avoid them.

"The happy couple!" the bartender shouts.

It's Strong Boy, one of Elwood's drinking buddies. He owns the Blue-Collar Barber Shop two blocks away. His head is shaved. His mustache is wide and black, greased and twisted to pointy ends.

"We'll be happier after a few drinks," I say.

He pulls a bottle of Marchel Foch from under the bar.

"You remembered!" Maggie says and kisses my cheek.

"His idea, too," Strong Boy says, as he pops the cork and fills two green plastic cups.

"Like the olden days," I say.

"That's right!" Maggie says. "We used to play Backgammon and drink red wine from green plastic cups."

I pull her close, "*I* liked it best *after* the games and drinking."

"Typical boy."

She stiffens. Pushes me away.

"But it feels like just yesterday."

"No, it feels longer."

"Is that good or bad?"

"It just *is*, honey."

The bottom of her dress is drenched and muddy, but the top is clean and white and tight to her body. Her skin glistens with raindrops. I kiss her neck, settle my hand into the small of her back and move it down, slowly. She reaches around and pulls it away.

"There's plenty of time for that," she says.

Lightning cracks. Thunder booms. Raindrops pound the metal roof. Maggie leans into me and we sway to the music of Captain Crayfish and the Musical Minnows, a group of old farts that have known Elwood since middle school. They cover country-western classics and butcher songs by Elvis Presley and The Doors. They are finishing up *Kiss an Angel Good Morning* when the Reverend stumbles between us with whiskey breath and rosy cheeks.

"A toast!" he says.

Maggie rolls her eyes. Eases away. Is quickly swallowed up by women that have been waiting to paw and pet, hug and kiss.

The Reverend slings a big, meaty arm around my shoulders. Shoves a flask into my face.

"In vino veritas," he says.

morning devils

Ten a.m. and ZuZu's still asleep, in her pink room, under yellow, glow-in-the-dark stars scattered across the ceiling. She's afloat in a sea of stuffed animals, comfy and warm under her fuzzy blue blanket with its silky ribbon trim pulled tight to her chin. Around her, the room blooms with Maggie's paintings—creations from the thirty-nine weeks and three days she carried baby ZuZu. Butterflies and bunnies. A fox, a cow, an otter. A turtle, a goat, a bear. Above her headboard hangs the family favorite: a ruby-throated hummingbird. Maggie's best, perhaps. Vibrant colors and loose shapes make it both real and dreamlike. The bird hovers above an enormous purple pitcher plant, its wings a blur of energy.

For Maggie, the painting is a childhood memory. Her Dad traveled for work selling industrial equipment to Chrysler, Ford, and GM. When he was home, he chose drinking, playing cards, hunting and fishing over family. Her Mom smoked and drank. Cleaned and baked. She volunteered at the animal shelter, gardened, got paid to write greeting card verse, and quietly battled constant fatigue that turned out to be cancer. Nobody knew or cared until it was too late. When she was gone, her Dad ran through as many of the town's women as he could. He suffered not one stroke, but two, had a triple bypass, and an ICD placed in his chest. This slowed him for a month, maybe two. Then he was back at it. Bad decisions daily. Maggie distanced—fourteen going on thirty. During the school year, she buried herself in homework and housework. In summer, she spent time with friends doing everything or nothing at all. But her favorite moments were those spent alone. At home, on the deck, sipping Faygo Redpop, drawing and painting while hummingbirds zipped back and forth between feeders in the yard.

For ZuZu, the bird is Daniel. She talks to him before bed. I've heard it many times. Usually after pouring a giant nightcap and passing her door on my way to the den to write. She relays the events of her day. Shares secrets, hopes, worries, good news, and bad. I hear bits and pieces but never stay long enough to know more than I should. That's her time. Those are her thoughts. I know what it's like—the need to be alone. To release without judgment. I'm happy ZuZu learned this so soon. Just letting go.

At the living room window, I sip my second Bloody Mary and think of the hummingbird painting. To me, it is balance. Harmony. A plant feeding silently. Building strength one dead insect, one drop of water, one ray of sunshine at a time. It waits, grows, and knows that if it is patient and still—oblivious to time—the hummingbird will come too close. Be too curious. And then, as a reward for all its patience and sacrifice, the pitcher plant will have its great chance to swallow the bird whole. This thought makes me smile and heave a great sigh as I watch the big white sun slowly rise.

Chickadees, blue jays, and sparrows take turns at the feeder. Below them, a fat gray squirrel stuffs his bulging cheeks. Then come two big, black grackles. Noisy, disruptive, muscling their way in. The other birds scatter. Even the squirrel flees, bounding toward the giant maple in the corner of the yard. The grackles shimmer blue, green, purple. Their golden eyes gleam—deceptive, brilliant. They caw like crows, screech like blue jays, and meow like cats. They raid nests to break eggs and eat the unborn. They toss hatchlings from trees then swoop down to devour them. But as devilish as they seem they are only playing their part. Nature is brutal. Survival is not guaranteed—not to the weak, the strong, not to anyone or anything at all.

The Bloody Marys are humming now. Vibrating my veins. Steadying me. I take a long drink, savor the salt and the pepper, the kick of the Tabasco sauce and the bite of the Sobieski, and find calm. I'm warm. Human once more. I tap the window with my fist. The grackles fly off, and all of us are safe, for now.

maple hills

Bright stars glint and twinkle. In the distance, planes roar, coming and going from Detroit Metro. We are on the front porch. Seven years and 257 miles from where it began. Words making white vapor in the evening's cold air.

"South Dakota?" I ask. "What's in South Dakota?"

"An art studio," Maggie says.

"You have one on the island."

"Take it," she says. "After it's empty, of course."

"So, you're going to load up my kid, a life of artwork, and move to South Dakota?"

"Sioux Falls," she says.

ZuZu wraps herself around my leg. Our eyes meet. She's tired. I'm tired.

"I don't want South Dakota," she says.

"Nobody wants South Dakota, Zu," I say.

Maggie leans against the house. Sighs. A brown curl falls and dangles between her eyes. Like magic, she manifests an orange scrunchie from nowhere, reaches up with both hands, and pulls the fallen curl and everything else back. Her jean jacket opens to reveal Frank Sinatra's mug shot from 1938. My T-shirt. One she bought for me six Christmases ago.

"I want to go to South Dakota," she snarks. "To Sioux Falls. With our kid. You, as usual, will be doing your thing, on the island for God-knows-how-long. Maybe through winter?"

"Set up in Thunder Bay, then. At the cottage."

Maggie rolls her eyes. Crosses her arms.

"I don't think so."

"You'll have your own space. And then, it's not that long of a drive," I say, nodding toward ZuZu. "For visits and such."

"Ninety minutes," Maggie says. "Then twenty-five minutes of ferry."

"I love the ferry!" ZuZu exclaims. "The island too! I like when the horses take us up the hill in the buggy!"

Maggie moves closer, then kneels to get level with ZuZu. I breathe. Slowly. Deeply. And there it is—grapefruit and bergamot. The same sweet scent from hugs we used to share—good morning, good afternoon, goodnight.

"I know, honey. I like the island too. But Daddy and I have a lot to discuss."

"Oh, no..." ZuZu says, and scoots across the porch away from us, "More discussing."

My phone CHA-CHINGS! like an old-fashioned cash register.

ZuZu leaps to her feet, "Greta! Greta! Greta!" she cheers.

I'm at The New Hudson Inn, the text reads. Thinking about my favorite writer. Meet me for drinks?

We're a long way from that cold December day when Greta Gellhorn, a recent graduate student and owner-operator of upstart Apple Tree Agency, found a 75-cent copy of my self-published book, *Dead Bunnies*, at Bicycle Bookshop in Kalamazoo and decided to represent me.

"Well, what did she say?" Maggie asks.

"Book signings. Updated numbers. I hate that shit."

ZuZu stomps her foot. Scowls. "Don't swear, Daddy!"

"And don't hate it," Maggie says. "Not long ago you were writing from a basement in the projects, and we were struggling to make ends meet."

"I'd go back if I could," I say it. Immediately regret it.

Maggie bites her lip. Nearly loses it to tears and crying and everything else that's balled up and ready to spring out from inside. It's awful seeing her like this on the porch where we used to sit and drink wine and watch ZuZu chase moths and grasshoppers. Where we talked and listened as the big sun slipped down behind the maples night after night to meet the horizon. She has something to say. It's on the tip of her tongue. But she will not let it out to be free and run, and I don't know how to help. Communication, intimacy, everything I thought we would always share has been lost in roles and expectations, and it is our inability to share and explain and get it all out—to get it back—that heightens my pulse, sends my heart into my guts, and makes me wish she didn't look so pretty—even now, with darkness all around and sadness in her face—and that we weren't falling apart like this in the middle of our life.

Maggie wipes her eyes, and there is a great sparkle as her diamond catches the light.

"You're still wearing it," I say.

"I'm still married."

She is on shaky ground now.

ZuZu walks over and takes her hand. Maggie smiles. Lifts her. They hug.

"I don't want South Dakota, Mommy."

"I know, honey," Maggie says. "I know."

And then they bring the tears, lots of them, but I don't want any, so I focus on the flashing lights of planes pushing through the dark sky, and I think of the men and women, husbands and wives—some of them great distances from home, great distances from themselves and each other—traveling together or alone. People with more disaster, fear, and failure stitching together their relationships—their lives—than any outsider could ever know. And I wonder, if people trust strangers to land them safely from flights so high above the earth, why can't Maggie and I even get off the ground?

"I don't want South Dakota," ZuZu says.

I head this off before it goes too far.

"Let's not worry about South Dakota. Let's worry about Frankenmuth."

"I thought you were going to the Detroit Zoo?" Maggie asks.

ZuZu jumps from Maggie's arms. Stands between us. Wipes her eyes with her arm.

"What's Frankenmuth?" she asks.

"Frankenmuth is a town. About ninety minutes north."

"But I want to see polar bears," she says.

"We'll see bears."

"We will?"

"Sure, black bears, and there'll be a tiger and lion, and—"

"But I want the glass cave. The tunnel with the water around us where we watch bears swim."

"The Arctic Ring of Life," Maggie interjects, "Mommy remembers."

"Yes!" ZuZu shouts. "We can watch blind sea lions too. They swim and play with the big red ball."

"That's always fun," Maggie says.

"We're not going to the big zoo," I say. "We're going to a little zoo where we can feed goats and turtles and bunnies."

"Turtles!" ZuZu cheers. "Turtles, Mommy!"

"They have lots of shops too. Ice cream shops, candy shops, sausage shops, cheese shops, smoothie shops. We can eat and drink whatever we want."

Maggie glares at me, "Not too much drinking."

"Okay! Okay!" ZuZu cheers. "Let's go!"

I pick her up, we hug, and Maggie steps closer. She touches my arm, and for a split second, we are home. Husband and wife and daughter. On our porch. Decompressing from the day. All we need is a little wine, the birds, and the light of the sun, even if only for a few minutes before it disappears with no promise of a return.

"Where are you staying tonight?" I ask.

She takes her keys from her pocket. Backs away.

"Canton."

"What's in Canton?"

She pecks ZuZu's cheek.

"Friends," she says, and turns away.

My stomach boils.

"Bye, Momma!"

"Bye, honey!" Maggie sings back. "Love you! See you in four days."

ZuZu hugs me tight. Maggie walks away. Down the porch steps where we used to sit and feed breadcrumbs to the family of mallards that adopted us for three summers. Into the driveway where we played basketball and hopscotch. And into the 4Runner that took us everywhere. Grocery shopping at

Meijer. To Wasabi in Westland. To Hines Park. Red Robin. The Drive-In on Ford Avenue. Tigers' games. Bald Mountain in Lake Orion. And no matter the season, always up north to Thunder Bay. The place we swore we'd return to and live one day.

"I still don't want South Dakota," ZuZu says.

"South Dakota's not so bad. Mount Rushmore's there."

"Dead presidents in rock?"

"A great American landmark."

She rolls her eyes.

"You're a landmark."

"I'm Presidential material."

"Not even close," ZuZu says. "Besides, Mom's President."

She hugs my neck, and we watch Maggie's taillights until they're eaten up by the dark.

our summer cottage

Driving down Long Lake Highway. Excited and chatting about the little red cottage we just toured. The kids love it. I sense nothing but good vibes. But Sophie, my wife, doesn't like the neighbors so close, the shallow water at end of the dock, and that there are rocks, big jagged ones, just below the surface. To me, for the price and the condition of the property, I'm sold. You don't find waterfront cottages in Northeastern Lower Michigan for a song. And this place is singing.

"I think it's great," I say. "Just enough space, a low-maintenance yard, and a new roof."

"But those neighbors are right on top of us, and I know you. You'll be fighting with them in no time."

"Daddy doesn't fight," Ada says.

My daughter. Seven, curly blond, perpetually barefoot, and already in pursuit of a lofty life goal—to hug every creature, from bugs to blue whales, in the world. For now, it's only practice. JoJo the stuffed goat is clutched to her chest.

"He fights," Caleb says. "Remember the soccer game? He beat up Jared's dad."

My son—eleven, athletic, charismatic—and far too severe for his age. Always listening. Watching. Like today. No matter when I look in the rearview mirror, his steady blue eyes are on me.

"That was different," Sophie says. "And that's not the type of fighting I'm talking about."

"Daddy saved Jared," Ada says.

"Tell that to the cops," Caleb says.

I say nothing because there's nothing to say. I was handcuffed and put into a cruiser. *To calm down*, the officer said. Because I *really did a number on him.* The *him* being Tank Allen Bradford, Jared's Dad, a repeat offender out on parole for doing unsavory things to men, women, and children—theft, assault, aggravated battery. But apparently, he'd never crossed paths with a tired, overworked, undersexed, hungry father and husband. And so, when he hit Jared upside

41

the head, not once, but twice for letting three goals slide by him in the first half of a soccer game, I walked over—hotdog and coffee in hand—and said, *Hey, fucko, knock it off.*

Whatever happened next is gone. Later that night, Sophie and I drank wine and watched the kids jump and fight on the trampoline in the back yard.

"Quite the show, today," she said.

"That's what I hear."

"You really don't remember?"

"I just wanted a hot dog, a coffee, and to watch Caleb's game."

Sophie waved little flies away from her glass, took a drink. Sighed.

"It was all so wrong. Happening like that at a game. For kids."

Ours, now getting along, bounced in synchronicity. Higher and higher. Flapping their arms like birds. I drank the rest of my wine, little flies and all. I stood up, dizzy. My swollen hand throbbed.

"Need more wine?" I asked.

"I do," she said. "I'm still trying to come down."

"I'm sorry. It was a mess."

"It was. As soon as I saw him hit Jared, I knew it would be bad."

A butterfly appeared between us. Bright silvery blue wings with black edges. It floated up then flew around and over top of the trampoline. Caleb and Ada didn't notice.

"Something seized me," I said. "Like something jumped in, did the work, then jumped out."

Sophie looked up at me. Smiled. Then went back to watching the kids.

"He slapped you," she said. "Not once, but twice. You didn't flinch. You even set down your hot dog and coffee."

"I was so hungry. And I love that coffee there from that little yellow vendor truck."

I could feel my throat tightening. My mouth drying up while tears started making their way up from wherever it is the hurt keeps them stored.

She finished her wine. Handed me the empty glass.

"Once you started, I knew you weren't going to stop."

"I'm sorry. I don't know what happened. I..."

"It's okay," she said. "You did the right thing. We all get what we deserve."

And Jared's Dad got just that—25 years to life without parole in I-Max—Ionia, Michigan's home away from home for habitual violent offenders. Jared and his mother are safe, about as far away from him as they could get, in Rainbow, California. A small avocado and citrus town.

"I'm sorry, honey," Sophie says. "That's not the type of fighting I meant. I think that with the neighbors on top of us like that, it's a recipe for years of awkward encounters and odd situations. You aren't really a people person."

She squeezes my hand.

"And Ada's right, by the way," Sophie says, as she looks over her shoulder at Caleb. "Daddy did the right thing. He saved Jared."

"He nearly killed a man," Caleb says.

"Stop talking, Caleb!" Ada snips.

"Okay, let's just all zip it and focus on the cottage," I say. "Maybe not this cottage, but let's think of all of them that we looked at today. What did we like? What didn't we like? And we'll talk about it later over. Who's up for Pizza?"

"ME!" They all shout.

As we continue toward home, I'm deep into a daydream. Caught up in visions of my kids catching minnows and crayfish by the dock. Imagining all of us cruising the lake in a brand-new pontoon boat, smiling, warm, and happy. Me and Sophie being awful parents, sipping cocktails, as Ada and Caleb take turns steering the mighty vessel around the lake until we're all filled up on fresh air and sunshine. When we return to the cottage, Sophie and I sit side-by-side in clam back chairs under the starry sky listening to waves moving against the shoreline. The kids laugh as they run barefoot through the cool grass, chasing lightning bugs.

"David!" Sophie screams.

And here is the deer. Not a fawn exactly. More like an adolescent with spots.

I can't swerve left because there's a white car coming from the opposite direction. I can't swerve right because the shoulder is soft and narrow and the ditch is deep enough to send us flipping. All I can do is hit the brakes and brace for what's to come. A terrible thud and crunch. Bits of plastic flying. Sophie shrieking, Caleb crying, and Ada too short to see, but shouting, "What happened, Daddy? What happened?"

The Subaru grinds to a halt.

"Is everyone okay?"

"No!" Caleb says. "Everyone's not okay! You killed a deer!"

"Awww," Ada says.

I watch the white car in the rearview mirror. It slows but does not stop. It moves on, carrying its passengers away from the scene of an accident. Maybe they're busy, I think. Heading to look at a cottage on the lake.

Sophie has her hand clamped over her mouth. Caleb has his head in his lap and is covering his ears. Ada smiles at me as she fights back the tears.

I step out into the sunlight. The warm light feels sharp, cutting through my skin, and the sounds inside the car blur into the background. Gravel crunches underfoot as I move toward the deer.

When I get to it, it's clear that this will take much longer than a minute. There's a broken neck, busted ribs, and blood leaking from its mouth and nose. But the spinal cord must be intact because it's moving its eyes and twitching its legs.

I kneel and stroke its side. Apologize. The sunlight shifts. A vulture glides over. I glance back at the Subaru, but the glare bouncing off the windshield hides everything inside. There is nobody else here for this. Just me and the deer.

So, I pick it up and carry it to the woods. Its head dangles. Swings back-and-forth. The little body tremors as I navigate through brush and branches.

At a clearing near the base of a large cedar tree, I lay the deer on the ground. There is gurgling, more blood. The deer struggles to breathe. It could survive like this for hours, maybe the night, even a day, so I break boughs from the tree, place them over the deer's face, and shove my knee into the deer's throat.

I push and push as hard as I can. What I've started cannot be stopped. Not even as a twig snaps, and I turn to find myself locked in the glassy-eyed gaze of the big doe that's waiting for her baby.

bucket fish

Dad shows her the tricks.

Thread a #8 bronze hook through the middle of a cold, medium-sized nightcrawler. Bronze, to blend in. Cold, so it's lively. Medium, for presentation.

"The crawler dangles," he says. "Wriggles. Tries to swim. Gets nibbled up from both ends."

But she is distracted. He looks the same—white t-shirt, dirty jeans, sweat-stained Tigers cap pulled down tight, shading his eyes from the world—but he smells different. And he *feels* different. Not to touch. But in the air. She noticed at breakfast too. She cleared her plate of scrambled eggs and sausage links. He only got a forkful down. His hands trembled all morning until he filled and drank his silver travel mug empty. Twice.

Tap-tap-tap, he shows her, tugging the 4lb monofilament.

"This is how it feels."

He disappears with his mug. She holds the line between her thumb and forefinger. Lowers the squirming crawler into the dark green water. Watches it disappear between the bare blackened branches of someone's discarded Christmas tree. Strands of dirty silver tinsel wave with the current as she considers all that could be down there. And why.

He is back. Crouched and leaning over the bank, dipping a bucket into the river. He fills it halfway.

Tap. Tap. Tap. It comes. She yanks. Reels fast. And it is over.

"Great work!" he says. "And on your first cast!"

He tries to hug her. The same innocent Dad hug he's been giving for years. But he is damp. And sour. She pulls away.

"It wasn't a *cast*. I just put the stupid line in the water."

He unhooks the fish. Talks to it.

"She didn't even give you a fighting chance, did she?"

He drops it into the bucket. She snatches up the handle and storms off, rushing back to the campsite. The water sloshes. The fish swims in frantic circles.

"What's the matter?" he calls after her, gathering up the fishing gear.

Back at camp. Crickets chirp. Frogs peep. She sits on a stump. Knives in her belly. Bucket clenched between her knees.

He stares into the fire with droopy, bloodshot eyes. Sways back and forth. Sips from his mug until ice rattles. Then, he turns. Stumbles to the cooler near the woods. Disappears.

Something—an animal—breaks twigs in the woods. Her chest tightens. Back aches. She pulls the bucket closer. Crosses her arms. Watches the sunfish float in dirty water. Gills in. Gills out. And together, they wait for the big sky to finish its switch from light to dark. To put an end to all of this. Send him wandering too far. To the river. Then a gentle push. Not to kill. Only a little slip and struggle in the cold dark water. But, like always, he comes back. Shuffles his heavy feet through the dirt and stands over the fire. A shadowy doppelgänger, smiling.

burying mr. beasley

Meelah is red-eyed. Barefoot. Wearing Strawberry Shortcake pajamas. She clutches last year's Valentine's Day mailbox to her chest. Reddish-brown fur and pink and white cards from third-grade classmates stick out from the slot.

I've been outside. Waiting. Keeping busy. The lawn needs mowing. Birdfeeders need filling. Hedges need trimming. The flowers thirst for water.

"He's in here," she says, shaking the box.

I follow her through the yard. She picks the dewy, overgrown garden. Points to a weedy spot between the purple tulips and white snowdrops. I sink the shovel into the ground and dig. Earthworms, split into halves, writhe in the freshly turned soil. A big gray cloud covers the sun. We're engulfed in shadow.

"The tails die," she says. "But the heads have the heart and brain. They can survive."

I dig and dig some more.

"Mom taught me that," she says.

∞

My wife's been gone only three weeks. It's too soon for all this. We just put her in the ground. I tighten my grip on the handle. Focus on the task at hand. But it all starts coming anyway.

Weekend breakfasts. Her eggs and orange juice. My bacon and coffee. Meelah snuggled up on the couch watching *Bugs Bunny* with her best friend—the cinnamon ferret, Mr. Beasley.

Daily walks through the park. Me, pulling the wagon. Mr. Beasley swaddled in a blanket on Meelah's lap. My wife walking beside me. Patient. Calm. Answering every question she's asked by our little girl. About trees and birds, bugs and the breeze, and why there are so many more black squirrels than gray.

Stories at bedtime. Until heavy eyelids. A hug and a kiss. And Meelah turns Mr. Beasley over to my wife. She cradles him in her arms. Walks him downstairs to his kennel and tucks.

"Night, Beasley," she says, time and time again.

The latch rattles. The light switch flips. Then her footsteps, padding up the stairs. She washes and brushes and gargles, then slides under the covers. Drapes her arm over my chest. Nuzzles my cheek. And we sleep.

∞

Meelah sniffles. Kneels.

"I wish she was here."

I crouch beside her. The cloud passes. Sunlight beams.

"Me too."

A tear slides down my face. Falls into the dirt.

"We'll be okay," I say.

She nods. Brings a big, fresh breath of the newly changed world inside of her and places the box in the hole.

"Night, Beasley," she says.

hollow

We plan this. All of it. Best dates to conceive. Best months to give birth. What to eat. Drink. How to sleep. What to listen to. Watch for. Feel.

We spend hours scrutinizing dented gallon cans of mis-tints and OOPS-pre-mixed paints. Miles trolling nice neighborhoods nights before trash days for a dresser, a lamp, a crib, a rocking chair. Then weeks turning my writing room into a nursery.

She sells cookies and cakes, brownies and breads she bakes at home. I fill a steel thermos with coffee. Pack a tin lunch box with white bread bologna-cheese-and-mustard sandwiches. Then grind and polish metal parts at a machine shop from dark to dark.

We go to bed tired but happy. She sleeps on her left side, pillow between her knees, face buried into my shoulder. I lie on my back. Staring at the ceiling. Listening to her breathe. Imagining the little person we made taking root, growing, becoming everything.

It's the end of my shift on a Tuesday when she calls.

"I need you," she says. "Now."

The day is dying. Light giving way to dark. I drive too fast on snowy roads. Fiddling with the defroster, I hit a snowdrift and get pulled into a rut on the shoulder. I'm stuck for half an hour. Digging slush from under the rusty frame with bare hands. Rocking the car back and forth from D to R so hard I snap the top off the shifter. I sweat in the cold car. My red hands throb and burn. I'm sure that a county snowplow is going to end me. And I don't want that to be the story my child hears. So, I slam the gas pedal to the floor. Rev the engine until the temperature gauge bounces off H, the fan belt squeals, and antifreeze burns in the air. When the tires finally catch, I'm off like a rocket, blasting down the road, pushing bumper-high snow. I run red lights. Pass two stranded motorists. I don't stop until I'm home.

The house smells like a burnt batch of something. The kitchen windows are open. Cold air rushing in. The oven is ajar, still smoking. She's in the living room, on the rocking chair. Naked from the waist down. Knees pulled up to her chin. Red fingerprints stain the backs of her thighs.

"What took so long?" she asks.

I move to touch her. She pulls away. Fixes her eyes on the bloody towel crumpled on the floor in front of the flickering woodstove.

"I didn't know what to do," she says. "But I thought I should keep it warm."

A season passes, but we don't move on. We're stuck in the cold, always waiting. Dark sky after dark sky.

Flocks of geese honk overhead, broken by wind gusts. Struggling to carry on. Clouds wrestle, wringing rain onto our leaky roof. Drip, drip, drip. Rot and mildew creep in. Slow decay.

She sleeps upstairs. I spend nights in the nursery. Staring at the walls. Writing in a notebook. Asking questions.

If we'd chosen pink or blue instead of neutral green, would

we have spent our summer collecting baby clothes from garage sales? Picking names from the baby book? How many times would I have held my ear to her belly, listening to the magic? And what does it sound like anyway? So buoyant. So warm. Just waiting. To be so much more than this. The silence of a hollow place. Empty space. Between us. Around us. Within her.

mange

Touring a 1940's custom-built brick home in a neighborhood that feels better than we deserve. Dreaming. There's more space—the kids will have their own rooms and two floors to hide and seek. A fireplace—Sophie and I will drink wine, unwind, be warmed by flickering flames and glowing coals. Maybe get close enough for long enough to fill the other two bedrooms with kids. If not, there's a wide, sprawling basement with a den filled with shelves for books. I can read and write or nap in a tight-back leather club chair.

And then we see the coons. Three of them. An adult and two young. They don't look good. Mange has them. They wobble and shake thirty feet up, as if the cold air itself is too much. It's January. Broad daylight. Twenty-two degrees.

I say nothing, but Debbie, the realtor, does.

"Oh, there are the critters!" she beams.

Ada and James press their faces against the window, steaming it up as they *oooh* and *ahh* and *wow.* They're already claiming them. Naming them—*Momma Rosa, little Ralphie and Roscoe the runt.*

Sophie's eyes are wide and watery, watching. The babies shiver and sway on brittle limbs.

"They're trembling," she says, and ushers the kids toward the front door.

"They're just a little cold," the realtor says. "I'm sure Momma Rosa will get them tucked away and warmed up in no time."

Debbie is clueless or a liar. Both are not helpful.

"They've got mange," I say.

Her cell phone dings. She checks it.

"Oh, they'll be fine," she says. "Mother Nature has a way of working things out."

And she moves on. To Sophie and the kids. There's ample storage. Walk-in closets. Three full baths. One of them with a heated soaker tub and jets. Sophie nods politely. Feigns interest. She has checked out.

∞

"I think we'll get the loan," I say to Sophie later that night. We're sipping wine, watching *Walk the Line*.

"I think so too," she says.

"We're good people, I think."

"We are good," she says. "But I don't want that house."

"But it's everything we want."

Sophie pulls her knees up to her chest. Says nothing. Stares at Joaquin Phoenix as he riles up the inmates. Smashes a glass of yellow prison water on stage.

I move closer. Reach my arm out and around her. She's tight. Cold to touch.

"You want a blanket?"

"No, thank you."

"It was the mange, wasn't it?"

"It was, but it wasn't," she says. "I don't want the kids seeing a slow death play out in front of them like that."

"The kids won't see it, honey."

She takes a sip. Softens a bit.

"Kids see everything."

"Even if it's not there?"

She puts her head on my shoulder.

"*Especially* when it's not there."

Joaquin becomes Johnny Cash right before our eyes. The inmates believe it. The warden believes it. Even I can't tell the difference anymore.

"Johnny goddamned Cash," I say.

Sophie smiles.

"What about him?"

"People these days don't get it," I say.

"Get what?"

"Anything. People just don't get it."

She puts her hand on my leg. Gives it a gentle pat.

"Like Debbie the realtor?"

"Just like Debbie," I say. "She doesn't get it. Doesn't even know what she's trying to sell. It's not just an old brick house. It's more."

"You okay, honey?"

Sophie moves closer. She's warm now. Cozy.

"I understand. No house. Not yet. Not this time."

She empties her glass. Takes mine and drinks it clean. Slowly, she pushes me back onto the couch. Lays over me—soft, melting. And holds her ear to my chest and listens to everything. Oxygen in. Out. Blood shooshing through capillaries and veins. And even my thoughts—in the basement of a better neighborhood, held by the comfort of a big, leather chair. Surrounded by books. My kids thumping up and down stairs. And my wife's light steps. Back and forth from fireplace to kitchen. Checking to see if raccoons with mange can make it through the winter.

glow

Sunshine breaks over the hardwood horizon. Maple syrup slowly rolls over pancakes. Soaks them through. Puddles all around on the plate. My stomach rumbles, but I can't bring myself to lift the fork. Instead, I stare through mist at a short-eared owl that sits atop the rusting swing set in the backyard. This is new. A blip in the cycle. It stays, staring at the house, for as long as I am at the table. Waiting for something I cannot see. I walk to the kitchen to scrape another morning of uneaten breakfast into the trash. Mix a drink. And when I return to the window, it is gone. If it was ever really here at all.

∞

I stumble outside at midday. Barefoot and buzzed. Into blinding white light. A black garbage bag of tiny clothes in one hand, pink plastic dollhouse in the other. To add to the growing pile. Dozens of stuffed animals. Puppy puzzles and mystery books. A purple dresser. Box spring. Twin mattress wrapped in Scooby Doo sheets. All of it mixed with waste—food scraps, unopened mail, unread newspapers, and empty bottles from ibuprofen, antacids, vodka, and B12. I stand staring at my feet. Moving my blue toes in the snow. Trying to remember how long I've been at this. In and out. Filling a gray dumpster with the wreckage of my life. Then I see it—sharp, crisscrossing talon marks, patches of gray fur, and red specks staining the snow. My belly tingles with warmth. I feel a flash of normal.

∞

Back inside it isn't long before I'm crazy again. Hidden away. Blinds drawn. Sipping Sobieski and 7UP. I pace the hallway past their empty bedrooms over and over until I no longer feel the need to look. I close their doors for good. Mix a drink. Settle into the couch to watch *It's a Wonderful Life*. And fall for Mary Bailey. All over again. She's devoted. Sings and dances. Never ages. And she always waits. Through idealism, selfishness, drunkenness. Great Depressions. And Christmas Eve tantrums. I see now why George reached the end of his rope in Martini's Bar and pled with God—desperate, teary-eyed, and trembling. I'd launch myself off a bridge too, simply to earn her forgiveness.

∞

This must be fiction—this loss. And this lack of reality is rooted in all I've been taught to believe. There is no magic, no sorcery, no talking with the dead. That's what the *Good Book* says. And as far as I can tell, all of this is scripted and proper. We are all, indeed, bitched from the start. And everything, no matter what, gets put where it's supposed to be. Me, remaining in place—a beast in my den. My wife, three states away, living in a city high-rise with a Bank Examiner. And my ten-year-old daughter in an orange urn. On their mantel.

∞

I drink myself so deep that I miss the change to dark. I'm startled awake by sound. Not the movie that's started again— stuck in a loop, like me—but a rumbling, then a thump, and pounding. In my head, my chest, the walls, the ceiling, and the floor. I rise, bleary-eyed and heavy, and stagger to the door. I open it and there is a man. Long hair, mustache and beard. Feminine build. He's wearing a Schwan's uniform. Says he's new on the route. That he's been waiting, was just about to leave but saw the flickering of the TV. He gives a spiel about holiday specials—spiral ham, roast turkey breast, green bean casserole.

"No," I shake my head. "Five boxes of buttermilk pancakes. One vanilla cup. Please."

A nametag hangs over his heart. *Jesus*, it says.

He smiles. I see a gold tooth.

"$34.18," he says with a barely perceptible wink. He turns and walks to the truck to fill my order.

The moon is white and full in the dark sky. Far too bright for me to handle. My eyes struggle as a gazillion stars pour light through the big, black canopy above. I rock side to side in the doorway.

"Thirty-four-eighteen, sir."

He sets the bag of goodies at my feet. Takes my credit

card. Sticks it into and pulls it out of his machine.

"$34.18," he says.

My stomach flutters.

"Why do you keep saying that?"

I feel weak. Steady myself against the doorframe.

"It's just the total, sir."

"No. No. I recognize it."

He smiles.

"I remember it. People said it would help. Bring peace. Understanding. I tried reading it like a novel front to back. That didn't work. Then in reverse. Back to front. Nothing clicked. I felt worse, but that...the 34:18. Which one is that?"

He offers nothing. Stares. Eyes blazing like fire. I feel myself faltering.

"From...from your book," I say.

Snowy wind blows up all around us. He hands me the receipt, but I let it fall and it floats off and away, like a moth into the night. I'm afraid I'll never have this chance again.

"Come on, man!" I shout. "I *know* you *know*! It's Psalms, right?"

He puts his hands on my shoulders. I close my eyes. The air turns woody and sweet, like Frankincense.

"The Lord is close to the brokenhearted," he says, then leans to whisper in my ear. "And saves those who are crushed in spirit."

When my eyes open, he is gone. Already climbing inside his chariot of treats. And when the door opens and the cab lights up, there is my little girl. She's in the passenger seat. Safe and warm. Smiling. She waves to me. I wave back. And for the first time in months, I glow.